La Marca Ysaguirre

Cold Dishes for Hot Weather

La Marca Ysaguirre

Cold Dishes for Hot Weather

ISBN/EAN: 9783337343064

Printed in Europe, USA, Canada, Australia, Japan

Cover: Foto ©Andreas Hilbeck / pixelio.de

More available books at **www.hansebooks.com**

COLD DISHES FOR HOT WEATHER

YSAGUIRRE AND LA MARCA

NEW YORK

HARPER & BROTHERS PUBLISHERS

1896

PREFACE

WHEN the hot midsummer months come, who is it that does not feel a repugnance for hot food, and whose palate does not demand something delicate yet cold? For them, and for the housekeeper who is so unfortunate as to have to attend to the culinary department of her establishment, is this book intended. All the receipts given are for dishes to be eaten cold; many of them require no cooking, as canned and preserved goods may be used in their preparation, although fresh meats and vegetables are always preferable; and all can be prepared in the cool morning hours, before the sun's rays make life hardly bearable.

The authors hope that this collection of receipts will be welcome, taking, as it does, the one unfilled place in the long list of culinary works.

THE AUTHORS.

April, 1896.

CONTENTS

INTRODUCTION

WE read in physiology that "many aromatic substances" and "various kinds of flesh when well cooked, especially when highly spiced or flavored with sauce, undoubtedly excite the stomach, and stimulate the appetite by their odor, and it is this that makes the artifices of cookery so valuable when the appetite is not naturally strong"; so that by going into the higher sciences—for cookery is a science in itself—we find the methods which should be followed by all cooks, and which the French long ago discovered and put to practical use, by which means a dish is made appetizing by giving it a flavor that shall not alone tickle our nostrils, but also excite our appetite by its fragrance.

As the appetite is excited by the sense of smell, so is it also by that of sight. A dish may be very fragrant, and also agreeable to the palate, but if the general appearance is not such as to please the organs of sight it will so counterbalance the sense of smell that, if the appetite of the person be not highly developed, the dish will be repugnant, and the diner unable to bring himself to eat it.

It naturally follows that the cook must be also an artist, both as to the aroma of his or her preparations and as to the artistic arrangement of the different dishes with which he or she would please the palate of the *gourmet*.

The authors believe that the receipts given will be—for their fragrance and taste—welcome, but they leave to the artistic ability of the cook to so garnish the different dishes as to make them pleasing to the sight.

All greens, such as cresses, parsley, lettuce, etc., and vegetables, such as beets, carrots, radishes, also eggs, and, in fact, one thousand and one things, will suggest themselves to the cook of artistic taste, which can be used to garnish the dishes with.

For desserts, fancily cut colored papers, Chinese paper napkins, narrow ribbons of bright colors, mottoes, etc., can be used to give an attractive appearance to the different dishes.

Consommé

Consommé should be strained very clear, and so served, or colored with a little burnt sugar or a piece of bread toasted. It may be taken as a liquid, or, as some people prefer, a jelly.

Very good soups and consommé may be bought in tins and jars at any of the principal grocers', but these, like all canned or preserved goods, lack that delicate flavor which can only be obtained from fresh goods.

CALF'S-FOOT CONSOMMÉ

Boil 2 calf's feet, 2 ounces veal, a little nutmeg, a few blades of mace, and salt to taste, in 3 quarts of water, till it is reduced to 3 pints; strain, take off the fat, and place on the ice to cool.

1

CHICKEN CONSOMMÉ

Boil a fowl, including the head and feet, nicely scalded and cleaned; add to the liquor a blade of mace and an onion; boil briskly till the meat separates from the bones; strain off and place on the ice to cool.

CONSOMMÉ OF MUTTON

Place 12 mutton shanks, 1 pound of lean beef, and an onion, with 4 quarts of water, in a saucepan, and allow to simmer for four hours. Strain off. When cold, place on the ice to harden, or it may be taken liquid.

CONSOMMÉ ROYAL

Boil briskly for an hour the head and feet of four fowls, 1 pound of lean beef cut into small pieces, in 2 quarts of water, and add an onion, turnip, and salt to taste. Remove the scum. Strain off and place on the ice to cool.

CONSOMMÉ OF VEAL

Take a knuckle of veal, a fowl, 4 shank bones, 3 blades of mace, a few pepper-corns, an onion, and boil in 3 quarts of water.

When it boils skim it till the scum ceases to rise, cover the vessel, and allow to simmer for four hours. Place on the ice to cool.

IMPERIAL CONSOMMÉ

Cut 2 pounds of lean veal into small pieces, adding half a pound of lean ham and a small chicken. Place in a stewpan with 1 ounce of butter, 3 onions, 2 carrots, 8 mushrooms, 1 celery stalk, 1 parsnip, a blade of mace, and a quarter of a pint of water; let it stew in the pan till it catches at the bottom and is quite brown, but not burnt, then add 4 quarts of water; let it boil gently for three hours, then strain off and place on the ice to cool.

WINDSOR CONSOMMÉ

Cut 4 pounds of beef into small slices; place a slice of lean undressed bacon on the bottom of the stewpan; lay the meat over it, with a few bits of butter or a cupful of fresh gravy. Slice over this a carrot, 2 onions, a little shallot, a stalk of celery, 2 bay-leaves, and some sweet herbs. Use a deep pot.

Place over the fire, and shake occasionally to prevent the meat from sticking. When the meat is browned on both sides, and the juice partly drawn, add the necessary amount of water, allowing for waste. Skim well, check the boil with cold water, and skim it again and again. Let it simmer for three hours; strain and place in a cool, dry place.

Fish

BAKED HERRINGS

SCALE, wash, and dry the herrings; mix some pepper, a few cloves, and salt; rub over the fish. Lay the herrings in a pot; cover them with vinegar; add a few bay-leaves; cover tightly. Bake in a moderate oven. Serve cold.

BAKED SALMON

(1.) Place the fish in a deep pan; put bits of butter over it. Season with allspice, mace, salt, and paprika; rub a little of the seasoning on the inside. Baste occasionally with the gravy that collects in the baking-pan. Serve cold; garnish with parsley.

(2.) Scale and dry a fresh salmon; take out the bone by splitting down the back; salt it well, and allow to stand till the brine is drained off; then season with mace, cloves, and a little red pepper, pounded fine; place the salmon in a covered pan, with bay-leaves, and cover it with butter; place in the oven, and when done drain it from the gravy. Allow to cool, and pour over clarified butter.

CAVEACH MACKEREL

Clean and divide 6 mackerel; cut each half into 3 pieces. Powder and mix 1 ounce of pepper, 2 nutmegs, a little mace, 4 cloves, and salt; make a hole in each piece of fish, into which force the seasoning. Fry in oil, allow to become perfectly cold, put in a stone jar, and cover with vinegar.

COLD CRABS

(1.) Pick the meat out from the shells and claws of boiled crabs; add some bread crumbs, paprika, essence of anchovy, 2 spoonfuls of vinegar, some clarified butter, and a spoonful of cider vinegar; mix thoroughly. Clean the shells and fill them with the mixture. Pound the spawn in a mortar, pass it through a sieve, and lay it over the crabs in fancy shapes. Garnish with parsley and the claws. The meat of two crabs will fill but one shell.

(2.) Pick out the meat; mix it well with a teaspoonful of salad-oil, red pepper, and salt. Serve in the shells.

COLLARED EEL

Bone a large eel, whole; lay it out flat, and season with pepper and salt, a table-spoonful of pounded mace, allspice, a table-spoonful of chopped parsley, a small onion chopped fine, thyme, and marjoram. Roll up the eel, beginning at the tail; tie in a cloth, and place in a stewpan, together with a gill of vinegar, a pint of water, an onion, and 2 bay-leaves; boil for an hour. When cold take off the cloth and keep it in the liquor in which it was boiled, adding to it a little salt.

COLLARED EELS

Mix together parsley, shallot, thyme, mar-joram, pepper, mace, cloves, nutmeg, allspice, powdered mushrooms, lemon-peel, and salt.

Clean and bone the eels; lay them flat, with the inside upward; rub the above mixture well into them. Roll them up and tie in a cloth; boil in salt and water, with lemon-peel, a few bay-leaves, and pepper; add some vinegar. When done take the collars out, skim off the fat, and boil down to a jelly, which is to be poured over the eels when cold.

COLLARED MACKEREL

Bone the mackerel, and sprinkle with salt, pepper, a tablespoonful of allspice, chopped onion, and parsley; roll them up and place in a pan; pour over them enough water and vinegar, mixed, to cover them; let them boil gently for an hour; keep them in the pickle, and serve cold. They may be baked instead of boiled.

COLLARED SALMON

Split, scale, and bone the salmon; season with mace, cloves, pepper, and salt; roll up in a cloth; bake it with butter and vinegar. Serve cold.

GENEVA SALMON

Tie up a piece of salmon, and place in a kettle with sliced onions, carrots, salt, spices, and a pint of claret or port; when done take from the liquor and serve cold with tartar sauce.

MOCK CAVIARE

Bone and pound some anchovies together with a little dried parsley, a clove of garlic, a little red pepper, salt, lemon-juice, and a little oil. Serve on toasted bread.

PICKLED OYSTERS

(1.) Wash the oysters; strain the liquor, and add to every pint a glass of white wine, mace, nutmeg, white pepper-corns, and salt; simmer the oysters for five minutes, but do not allow to boil, as they will become hard. Place them in glass jars. Add to the liquor a glass of vinegar, and boil; skim the pickle, and pour over the oysters. When cold cover very tightly.

(2.) Place the oysters in a stewpan; sprinkle with fine Lisbon sugar; add their liquor, well strained, and set on the fire for five minutes, but do not allow to boil. Draw off the liquor, and add to it double the amount of vinegar, together with some catsup, paprika, lemon-peel, and salt; boil a quarter of an hour. Sprinkle the oysters with sugar and salt, and place them in a stone jar. When cold strain the pickle over them and cover very tightly.

(3.) Put the oysters in a saucepan with their own liquor, and allow to simmer gently for ten minutes; then lay in a jar. When cold pour over them the following pickle: boil the liquor of the oysters with a bit of mace, lemon-peel, black pepper, and vinegar. Keep in small jar well covered.

PICKLED SMELTS

Wash and clean the smelts. Pound together half an ounce of pepper, half an ounce of mace, half an ounce of saltpetre, and the same quantity of nutmeg; lay the smelts in layers, placing the seasoning between each layer; add a few bay-leaves; boil some red wine, and pour over the fish enough to cover it. When cold cover well.

PICKLED STURGEON

Cut the sturgeon into small pieces; wash it well, and tie in a cloth. To 3 quarts of water add 1 quart of strong beer, salt, 1 ounce of ginger, 2 ounces of pepper, 1 ounce of cloves, and 1 ounce of Jamaica pepper; when the liquor boils put in the sturgeon; when done take it from the fire and allow to stand overnight; add a quart of strong vinegar and salt. Cover closely.

POTTED EEL

Skin and clean a large eel; dry and cut into small pieces about four inches in length; season with mace, pepper, and salt; lay in a pan and cover with melted butter; bake for half an hour in a quick oven. When done take it out and place on a cloth to drain. Pack closely in a pot; melt the butter it was baked in, and pour it over the eel.

POTTED HERRINGS

Cut the heads off the herrings and lay in

an earthen pot; sprinkle a little salt between each layer; add cloves, mace, pepper, and sliced nutmeg; fill up the vessel with vinegar, water, and white wine; cover it and place in the oven. When cold take out the herrings and put into well-covered vessels.

POTTED LOBSTER

(1.) Parboil the lobster; cut it into small pieces, and season with mace, white pepper, nutmeg, and salt; press into a pot and cover it with butter; bake for half an hour; put in the spawn. When cold take out the lobster and put it into covered vessels with a little of the butter; beat the rest of the butter with some of the spawn, and cover the lobster with it.

(2.) Take out the meat from the lobster without breaking; season with mace, nutmeg, white pepper, salt, and cloves. Put a little butter at the bottom of a pan, and lay the lobster over it, placing between the layers a few bay-leaves; cover with butter, and bake in a slow oven; when done strain, lay in potting-pans, and add the seasoning. When cold pour clarified butter over it.

POTTED MACKEREL

Clean, season, and bake the mackerel in a pan, with plenty of spices, bay-leaves, salt, and butter. When cold put them into a pot and cover with butter.

POTTED SALMON

Split, scale, and clean the salmon, but do not wash; rub with salt, and drain off the moisture; season with pounded mace, cloves, black pepper, and cayenne pepper. Cut the salmon into small pieces, lay them in a pan, and cover with melted butter. Bake, drain from the fat, put the pieces into pots and cover with clarified butter.

SALMAGUNDI

Wash and open 2 pickled herrings; remove the meat from the bones, being careful not to break the skin, and keeping the head, tail, and fins on it; mince the fish with the breast of a chicken, the yolks of 2 hard-boiled eggs, an onion, a boned anchovy, a little grated ham or tongue; season with oil, vinegar, red pepper, and salt; fill up the herring-skins so that they may look plump, and shape carefully. Garnish with parsley, and serve with mustard.

SALMON JELLY

Break the salmon into flakes; season with allspice, nutmeg, salt, and pepper; fill a mould with alternate layers of the salmon and aspic jelly. Turn out on a flat dish, and garnish with lettuce - leaves and hard-boiled eggs.

CEBICHE DE CAMARONES (CRAWFISH)

Boil the crawfish and remove the shells. Cut 3 onions into rounds; pour boiling water over them, let stand for five minutes, and repeat two or three times. Strain the juice of bitter oranges or lemons; mix in salt and paprika; put the fish into a deep dish together with the onions, and pour over them enough of the lemon - juice to completely cover them.

CEBICHE DE PESCADO (FISH)

Cut the fish into half-inch cubes. Prepare the onions as in the preceding receipt; also the lemon-juice, with the paprika and salt. Put the fish into a deep dish, with lemon-juice sufficient to cover it; allow to stand for three or four hours; stir well every ten minutes until the fish looks white and cooked. Bear in mind that the fish does not go near the fire. The best fish to use is halibut.

Meats

BEEF À LA MODE

(1.) TAKE 4 pounds of bottom round, and rub well with powdered spices and salt. Lay skewers on the bottom of the stewpan, and spread over them thin slices of bacon; place the beef on the bacon, and lay over it a few more slices; add a little vinegar; cover closely and stew for two hours. Add to the gravy a seasoning of cloves, pepper, bay-leaves, mushrooms, a little catsup, and a few button onions; simmer till the meat is quite tender; serve the meat dry; strain the gravy and boil it slowly for an hour, when it will jelly; glaze the meat with the jelly.

(2.) Slice and fry to a nice brown 2 onions; cut a quarter of a pound of bacon into small pieces; dip them into 3 tablespoonfuls of vinegar; make deep holes in a nice piece of beef weighing about 4 pounds, into which put the bacon; rub the beef well with allspice, cloves, 2 blades of mace, salt, pepper, a bunch of sweet herbs, all finely minced; place the beef in a saucepan; pour over it the vinegar, a small glass of currant jelly, the juice of a lemon; add a carrot, turnip, a head of celery, and the spices; allow to simmer gently for four or five hours. Take up and set on a dish to cool.

BEEF BOUILLI

Cut cold beef into slices about half an inch thick and about two inches wide; make a dressing of finely chopped shallots, parsley, pepper, salt, mustard, egg, oil, and vinegar; pour the mixture over the beef; serve garnished with water-cress.

COLLARED BEEF

Lard a piece of corned beef; make holes in it, and fill with a dressing of bread crumbs, suet, parsley, grated lemon-peel,

2

sweet herbs, pepper, salt, nutmeg, and the yolk of an egg mixed well together; bake with a little water, whole peppers, and an onion. Serve cold.

DAUBE GLACE

Take a piece of lean beef; make holes in it, and fill them with strips of fat which have previously been rolled in powdered sage, pepper, allspice, salt, and a little minced shallot. Boil 2 calf's feet to a jelly; strain and set aside to cool. Place the meat in a pan with the jelly; add to it some cloves; cover very tightly and cook for four hours. Place in a deep dish; pour the jelly over it; cool and put on the ice.

FORCED BEEF

Lard a piece of fresh corned beef; make holes in it, and fill them with bread crumbs, suet, parsley, grated lemon-peel, sweet herbs, pepper, salt, nutmeg, and the yolk of an egg, mixed so as to make a stuffing; bake in a pan with a little water and wine, whole pepper, 2 bay-leaves, and an onion. When done skim off the fat; put the meat in a dish and pour the liquor over it; set aside to cool.

GALANTINE OF BEEF

Mix together half a pound of bread crumbs, 1 pound of sausage meat, some chopped parsley, thyme, marjoram, seasoning, 6 eggs, and spice. Cut a piece of corned beef, weighing about 5 or 6 pounds, into a large thin sheet; season with pepper and salt; spread the force-meat over it; sprinkle some mushrooms over the meat, and roll it up very tightly; tie in a cloth, and boil on a slow fire for five hours; when done take it up and place between two dishes with a weight on top; when cold trim the ends and glaze.

JELLIED MEAT

Soak and clean 4 calf's feet; boil until done; strain and separate the meat from the bones, and set aside to cool; pour the liquor into a jar, and when cold remove the grease. Take a shank of beef and boil it until the meat falls in pieces; remove it from the liquor. Cut the meat from the calf's feet and the beef into small pieces; put the jelly into a pan; add to it the meat; mix well together, and heat to the boiling-point. Season with red pepper and salt to taste; pour into a mould to set.

POTTED BEEF

Take 4 pounds of corned beef; place in a pan with a little suet and water; cook in an oven; when done pound in a mortar till it is perfectly smooth; season with cayenne, salt, pepper, a little mace, some of the gravy, and half a pound of melted butter. When thoroughly mixed put into pots and cover with melted butter.

POTTED MEAT

Chop any kind of cold meat; season with salt, pepper, cloves, and cinnamon; moisten with a little wine, vinegar, and Worcestershire sauce. Pack the meat in a jar, and cover it with about half an inch of melted butter. This meat will keep for some time.

POTTED OX-TONGUE

Boil a fresh tongue; skin, clean, and re-move the bones; when cold mince very fine, and add 4 ounces of butter to each pound of tongue, some mace, nutmeg, cloves, paprika, salt, and a little black pepper; mix well; place in jars and pour melted butter over.

RED BEEF

Take a piece of corned beef and season it with pounded mace, cloves, pepper, a little allspice, salt, chopped parsley, and shallot. Boil it till tender; cut into thin slices; serve cold.

RIBS OF BEEF À LA PORCUPINE

Bone the flat ribs and beat them flat; rub over with the yolks of eggs; sprinkle on bread crumbs, parsley, leeks, marjoram, lemon-peel, nutmeg, pepper, salt, and a little paprika; roll it up very tightly; lard it with bacon; then a row of cold tongue, another of pickled cucumbers, a fourth row of lemon-peel; do it over in rows as above till it has been larded all over; then place in a deep pot with a little water; cook in a slow oven. Serve cold.

SPICED BEEF

Place 2 pounds of beef in a saucepan, together with one cupful of wine, the same quantity of water, 3 tablespoonfuls of vinegar, cinnamon, pepper, salt, and onions; cover the saucepan very tightly; place over a slow fire for two hours; take the meat from the gravy and set aside to cool.

VINAIGRETTE

(1.) Rub 1 teaspoonful of sugar, 1 tablespoonful of mustard, salt and pepper to taste, into the yolks of 2 eggs; add 3 tablespoonfuls of vinegar, set in a bain-marie, and cook until it is of the consistency of cream; allow to cool.   Boil 4 pounds of beef brisket until quite tender; when cold, dish on a flat plate and mask with the dressing; sprinkle over it chopped parsley, pickles, and a little shallot.

(2.) Place a piece of beef in a pan, and stew with a little water, a glass of wine, sweet herbs, an onion, bay-leaves, cloves, salt, and pepper; when done, strain the liquor, remove the fat carefully, and add a little vinegar; serve cold with the sauce.

COLLARED BREAST OF LAMB

• Bone the lamb, rub it over with the yolk of an egg, grate over it a little lemon-peel, nutmeg, pepper, and salt; chop up 2 tablespoonfuls of capers, 2 anchovies, some parsley, and a few sweet herbs; mix with bread crumbs, and spread over the lamb; roll it up, and boil two hours; take it up and put it into a pickle.

COLLARED NECK OF PORK

Bone the neck, and sprinkle with bread crumbs, chopped sage, a little allspice, some pepper and salt, mixed together. Roll it up close, and bind very tightly; roast for an hour and a half in a slow oven.

COLLARED SUCKING PIG

Bone the pig, rub it well with pepper, salt, a few sage leaves and sweet herbs chopped fine; roll up very tightly. Fill a pot with water, and add to it a bunch of sweet herbs, a few pepper-corns, a blade of mace, some cloves, salt to taste, and a pint of vinegar; when it comes to a boil put in the pig and allow it to boil till tender. When done take it up and cool; then place in a vessel and pour the liquor over it.

FORCED PIG'S EARS

Parboil 2 pairs of pig's ears; make a force-meat of an anchovy, sage, parsley, a quarter of a pound of chopped suet, bread crumbs, pepper, and a little salt; mix with the yolks of 2 eggs. Raise the skin of the upper part of the ears and stuff them with the force-meat. Fry the ears in butter, and drain them; make a rich gravy as follows: a glass of sherry, 3 teaspoonfuls of made mustard, a little butter, a small onion, a little pepper, and some paprika. Put the ears in a stew-pan with the gravy, and cover very closely; stew gently for half an hour. When done, strain the gravy and reduce to a jelly; place the ears on a dish and pour the jelly over them. When set, garnish with parsley.

SUCKING PIG AU PÈRE DUILLET

Cut off the head, quarter the body, lard it with bacon, and season with salt, pepper, nutmeg, cloves, and mace. Lay some fat bacon on the bottom of a pan, place the head in the centre, and arrange the quarters around it; add a bay-leaf, a chopped onion, a lemon, some carrots, parsley, and the liver; cover all with bacon; stew for an hour in a quart of stock, take it up, put in a stewpan, and pour over it a bottle of wine; simmer gently for an hour. Skim the fat off the first gravy; strain it; add to it a sweetbread cut into slices, some truffles, and mushrooms; stew the whole until it jellies; put the wine in which the pig was stewed into the jelly, pour it over the pig, and garnish with parsley.

BRAISED FOWL

Bone the fowl and stuff with force-meat. Fry a few slices of onions in a stewpan; add the bones and trimmings of the chicken, a bunch of herbs, a few blades of mace, and a pint of broth. Cover the chicken with slices of bacon, cover the pan very tightly, and stew for half an hour. Strain the braise gravy, and boil it up quickly to a jelly. Glaze the chicken with it, and serve cold.

CHICKEN CHEESE

Boil two chickens in a quart of water. When done take them out of the water and remove the bones. Mince the meat very fine together with 2 or 3 truffles, return to

the water, and cook until almost dry. Pour
into a deep dish, cover, and place a weight
on the cover. Put in a cool place.

CHICKEN JELLY

Pound half a raw chicken with the bones
and meat, cover it with cold water, and allow to simmer till the meat is reduced to
rags and the liquor to about half. Strain,
and pass through a very fine sieve. Salt
and pepper to taste. Return to the fire and
simmer for five minutes. Skim, and keep
in a cool place.

BRAISED DUCKS

Dress, singe, and lard with bacon a couple
of ducks. Season with parsley, mace, cloves,
pepper, and salt. Lay some slices of fat
bacon on the bottom of a stewpan; put in
the ducks with the breast downward; cover
them with slices of bacon; cut a carrot,
turnip, onion, and celery stalks; mix with
mace, four or five cloves, and pepper. Cover
well, and simmer over a slow fire till the
breasts of the ducks are of a light brown;

then put in some water, and cook till done. Chop very fine parsley, shallot, gherkins, capers, and 2 anchovies. Place in a stewpan with some of the liquor of the ducks, a little aspic jelly, and the juice of a small lemon. Boil it. Lay the ducks on a dish, pour over them the sauce, and serve cold. The sauce will form a glaze over the ducks.

GOOSE MARINADED

Bone and stuff with the following mixture: 12 sage-leaves, 2 large onions, 2 apples; chop fine and mix with bread crumbs, 4 ounces of beef suet, a glass of port, half a grated nutmeg, pepper, salt, grated lemon-peel, and the yolks of 4 eggs. Stuff the goose, sew it up, and fry till it is light brown. Put into a stewpan with 2 quarts of broth, cover closely, and stew for two hours. Take out the goose, and allow to cool. Take the fat from the gravy and add a tablespoonful of lemon pickle, port, an anchovy, mace, pepper, and salt. Allow to boil till reduced to a jelly, pour over the goose, and allow to cool. Garnish with beets cut into fancy shapes and sprigs of parsley.

PIGEON CUTLETS

Cut off the breasts and wings of six pigeons; flatten them out and trim in the shape of cutlets. Fry in butter, a tablespoonful of chopped parsley, an onion, and 2 or 3 button mushrooms, and pour over the pigeons. Season them with salt and pepper, dip in egg and roll in bread crumbs; fry in butter, and serve cold with tartar sauce.

PIGEONS IN JELLY

(1.) Boil a calf's foot. Put the broth in a pan with a blade of mace, a bunch of sweet herbs, pepper, salt, lemon-peel, a slice of lean bacon, and the pigeons. Bake them. When done, take them out and allow to cool. Clarify the jelly with the whites of 2 eggs, and strain it through a thick cloth. Put the jelly over the pigeons, and garnish.

(2.) Pick and roast two pigeons. Make a jelly as in the preceding receipt, and with it half fill a deep bowl. When the jelly and the birds are cold, lay the birds breast down in the jelly, and pour the rest of it over them, so as to completely cover them. When hard, turn out on a flat plate or dish, and garnish with parsley.

PUPTON PIGEONS

Make some force-meat; roll it out like paste, put it in a buttered dish, and lay over it thin slices of bacon, squabs, sliced sweet-breads, asparagus tips, mushrooms, and hard-boiled eggs. Put another layer of force-meat over the whole. Bake it, and when done turn it out into a dish. Serve cold.

TURKEY IN JELLY

Bone a turkey and stuff it with force-meat, to which add 6 truffles and 12 mushrooms. Lard it with fat bacon; tie it up; put in a pan just large enough to hold it. Add 2 quarts of strong stock, and stew for three hours. Allow it to cool; take the fat off the gravy. Dish the turkey, and pour the jelly over it.

FLORENTINE HARE

BONE a hare, except the head; make a stuffing of bread crumbs, the chopped liver, half a pound of bacon, a glass of red wine, an anchovy, 2 eggs, a little sweet-marjoram, thyme, salt, pepper, and nutmeg; fill the hare with the stuffing, being careful to force it up to the head; sew the opening, tie in a cloth, and boil for an hour and a half in two quarts of water; when reduced to half add a pint of port, a tablespoonful of lemon-juice, and one of catsup. When done, take out the hare and allow to cool; fill the eyes with a little piece of beet, and place sprigs of parsley in the mouth. Reduce the liquor to half a pint, or until it jellies; pour over the hare; garnish with rounds of hard-boiled eggs, beets, and sprigs of parsley.

LARDED HARE

Bone a hare, lay it flat on a board, and season with pepper, spices, chopped mushrooms, parsley, thyme, and shallots; spread force-meat over it, roll it up very tightly, and lard it with bacon. Put the bones and some ham into a stewpan with a few bay-leaves, onions, thyme, parsley, a few blades of mace, and half a pint of port; cover the bones with fat bacon, put in the hare, and cover it also with bacon; set on a slow fire to simmer for two hours; take out the hare, and allow to cool; glaze with aspic jelly; garnish with parsley.

PARTRIDGES À LA FRANÇAISE

Truss the partridges and skewer them; cover the breasts with slices of lemon, and over them lay some fat bacon; wrap them in paper and tie tightly. Roast for three-quarters of an hour; when done take off the paper and serve cold with the juice of Seville oranges.

POTTED PARTRIDGES

(1.) Truss the partridges; season inside with salt and pepper; place in a stewpan lined with slices of lean ham; add a bunch of thyme, some whole pepper, and allspice; cover with slices of ham; add a pint of water; cover tightly and stew for two hours; keep in the pot till cold, then put into pots with a few whole pepper-corns; pour clarified butter over them and cover tightly till used.

(2.) Clean the partridges, and season with mace, allspice, pepper, and salt; lay them breast downwards on a pan; pack the birds as close as possible; add plenty of butter; cover the pan very well and bake. When cold put the birds in pots and cover with butter.

POTTED RABBITS

Cut up 2 young rabbits, and take the leg bones out at the thigh; pack in a small pan and season with finely chopped pepper, mace, cayenne, and allspice; add plenty of butter, and bake gently. Keep in the pan for two days; then place in the pots and cover with clarified butter.

RABBITS EN GALANTINE

Bone and flatten out 2 young rabbits; lay force-meat upon them, slices of ham, and egg omelets; roll up tight and fasten them; lard with fat bacon; cook in a slow oven, and serve cold; glaze with aspic jelly colored with beet juice; garnish with parsley.

RABBITS À LA PORTUGUESE

Bone 2 rabbits, and spread force-meat over them. Put the bones in a stewpan with some onions, a few sweet herbs, a little mace, and a few bay-leaves; lay the rabbits over this and cover them with bacon; pour over a pint of stock and set the pan on the fire; simmer very slowly for an hour; strain off the liquor, remove the fat, and boil the sauce to a jelly; add to it a few truffles chopped fine. Serve the rabbits, and when cold glaze them with the jelly.

Vegetables

ALMOST every variety of vegetables can be eaten cold; and as the manner of preparing them is not unlike that of salads, but few receipts are given.

ARTICHOKE BOTTOMS

Boil 6 artichoke bottoms in salt and water; when done take them out and remove the chokes; boil till tender, and allow to cool. Spread some anchovy paste over each, and mask with a mayonnaise dressing; garnish with hard-boiled eggs and capers.

ASPARAGUS

Drain a can of asparagus tips and wash in cold water. Fresh asparagus may be used if preferred. Place the asparagus on ice, and serve with oil, vinegar, salt, and pepper.

BEETS

Cook and peel the beets; when cold cut into rounds, place in a deep dish, and cover with vinegar; add a little salt.

CUCUMBERS

Cut large cucumbers into rounds; place on ice; serve with salt, pepper, oil, and vinegar. Tomatoes may be prepared in the same manner.

ONIONS

Cut the onions into rounds, and pour boiling water over them; allow to stand for five minutes; then throw off the water. This will do away with the strong odor and bring out the delicate flavor. Place the onions in a deep dish and cover with vinegar; season with red peppers cut into strips and salt.

Bouchées

ANCHOVY BUTTER

WASH, bone, and pound 6 anchovies, adding sufficient butter to make a paste; scald some parsley and rub it through a sieve; mix the ingredients well; spread the butter on toast, and garnish with parsley.

ANCHOVY CANAPÉS

Scale and wipe dry some oil-preserved anchovies; cut them into long strips; wrap each strip in a piece of pastry, being careful to close the ends; fry in very hot lard. Dish, and sprinkle a little grated Parmesan cheese over them while hot; let cool, and garnish with lettuce-leaves.

ANCHOVY CREAM

Wash, bone, and pound 9 anchovies together with the yolk of a hard-boiled egg, 1 tablespoonful of oil, a little cayenne, and a few drops of carmine; when quite smooth mix in two tablespoonfuls of liquid aspic, and rub through a sieve; add two table-spoonfuls of whipped cream, and set aside till needed.

ANCHOVY CROÛTONS

Pound the yolks of two hard-boiled eggs, 1 ounce of butter, 1 teaspoonful of anchovy essence, and paprika to taste; pass through a very fine sieve, and add 2 boned anchovies pounded to a paste; mix well and spread on thin rounds of brown bread or toast. Garnish with strips of green and red peppers.

ANCHOVY FINGERS

Rub two ounces of butter and 6 of flour till quite smooth; add 1 teaspoonful of anchovy essence, cayenne, a well-beaten egg, and enough cold water to make a nice light paste; roll out very thin, prick it with a fork, cut it in strips, and bake in a moderate oven. When cold make sandwiches of the fingers, placing anchovy butter between

them. Brush the top over with a little aspic
jelly; before it becomes hard, sprinkle some
of the fingers with finely minced parsley,
others with the yolk of a hard-boiled egg
passed through a sieve, and the remainder
with the white of the egg finely chopped.
When the jelly has become quite firm, garnish with lettuce-leaves and serve.

CAVIARE BOUCHÉES

Cut small circles of bread and brown them
in butter. Chop together to a paste some
cress, nicely picked and dried, and the same
quantity of butter; mix well and spread a
little on each toast; spread some caviare on
top of this and garnish with parsley.

DUCHESS BOUCHÉES

Mix equal parts of curry-powder, powdered
truffles, bread crumbs, and browned flour;
add the yolk of a hard-boiled egg, grated
rind of half a lemon, 1 tablespoonful of Chili
sauce, a little butter, and 1 teaspoonful of
lemon-juice. Season with salt, red pepper,
and nutmeg to taste; stir this over a slow

fire until quite brown and thick; cool, and serve on small toasts or crackers.

DEVILED EGGS

Boil until hard 6 eggs; when cool shell and divide in half; remove the yolks and mix them with the same quantity of deviled ham; refill the whites. Dish in a nest of lettuce-leaves, and garnish with beet cut into fancy shapes.

EGGS À LA INFANTA

Boil until hard 6 eggs; shell and cut in half lengthwise; remove the yolks, being careful not to break the whites. Pound the yolks smooth, and mix with half a pint of mayonnaise dressing. Make a nest of lettuce-leaves, and place the whites on it; fill them with the yolks and mayonnaise. Garnish with capers and a beet cut into fancy shapes.

PARISIAN CANAPÉS

Cut small oblongs of stale bread, and fry in butter to a light brown; place on a piece of paper to cool—the paper will also absorb all the butter. Spread each piece with anchovy butter, and place on each a boned anchovy; sprinkle over them finely chopped olives mixed with a little chopped chives.

Pies and Patties

THE cost and trouble of making patty-cases is such that it is far preferable to buy them at the caterers'; especially is it desirable, as then the cook will not run the risk of spoiling the paste.

Pie pastry is not so easily spoiled as patty or puff paste, and as this is not obtainable, the cook will have to tempt fate and try her own skill at making it herself.

CHICKEN PATTIES

Cut the white meat of a chicken into small pieces. Place in a saucepan half a pint of stock and 2 ounces of lean ham chopped fine; let simmer. Mix a spoonful of butter and one of flour. Boil the broth to about half the original quantity; strain into a half-pint measure and fill up with cream; stir this into the flour and butter; when thick add the chicken. Keep at the boiling-point for five or six minutes; set aside to cool; when cold fill the patty-cases; garnish with sprigs of parsley.

CHESHIRE PORK PIE

Skin a loin of pork; cut into small steaks; season with salt, nutmeg, and pepper. Make a pie-crust, and fill with a layer of pork, then one of apples, pared and cored, and sugar enough to sweeten it, then another layer of pork; pour over half a pint of white wine, and cover all with a little butter before covering the pie. Serve cold.

HAM-AND-VEAL PATTIES

Chop 6 ounces of lean veal, 3 ounces of ham; put into a stewpan with 1 ounce of butter rolled in flour, 2 tablespoonfuls of cream, 2 tablespoonfuls of veal stock, nutmeg, a little lemon-peel, paprika, salt, and lemon-juice. Stir over fire, and when cold fill the patty-cases.

MINCE PATTIES

Chop a cold veal kidney and some fat; add an apple, orange, candied lemon-peel, fresh currants, a little wine, cloves, brandy, and sugar. Fill the patty-cases, bake, and serve cold.

OX-CHEEK PIE

Line a deep dish with puff-paste. Boil the ox-cheek with seasoning; cut into small pieces; lay in the dish, and throw over them 1 ounce truffles, the yolks of 3 hard-boiled eggs, a cup of mushroom pickles, half a cup of asparagus tips, and several force-meat balls. Season with pepper and salt, and fill up the pie with the gravy in which the cheek was boiled. Cover it with the crust, and place in the oven; when done allow to cool.

PRINCESS PATTIES

Fill the patty-cases with the following mixture: place 1 pint stock broth, half a pint of milk, seasoning, a little grated nutmeg, and thyme in a saucepan; boil for five minutes, then add a little roux and the liquor from 1 tin of mushrooms; boil until it becomes thick. Chop the meat of a fowl, half a pound of lean ham, and mushrooms finely, then add to the sauce; simmer a little while; then cool.

SAVORY ROLLS

Place in a saucepan 1 ounce of butter, a little shallot, sweet herbs, and parsley chopped fine; fry slowly for five minutes; then add 1 pint broth, some seasoning, the liquor from 1 tin mushrooms, and 2 pounds of rump steak; simmer for an hour, then take out the steak, and thicken the gravy with a little roux; boil three minutes. Chop the mushrooms, steak, and 4 hard-boiled eggs finely; stir gently into the sauce; allow to cool. Roll out some puff-paste very thin and cut into four-inch squares; place a little of the mixture in the centre of each, touch the edges with egg, fold over, and pinch the edges together; place on a baking-tin and bake a light brown. Serve cold.

SAUSAGE ROLLS

Cut three-quarters of a pound of pork and 3 ounces of fat into small pieces and mince, adding salt, pepper, mace, and allspice; spread on a board, and add 3 ounces of bread crumbs and seasoning; mix well. Roll puff-paste out to about a quarter of an inch, cut into squares, put some of the mixture on each square, wet the edges, fold over the meat, press the edges together, brush over with the yolk of an egg, and bake in a moderate oven.

SHEEP'S-HEAD PIE

Lay a sheep's head in salt and water overnight; wash it thoroughly with warm water; take out the soft bones from the nostrils; boil it till it is tender; chop the meat, together with half a pound of bacon and 1 hard-boiled egg; then add salt, pepper, some finely minced parsley, with half a pint of the liquor in which the head was boiled; put in a pie-dish, and cover with a short crust; bake in a moderate oven.

SWEETBREAD PIE

Lay a puff-paste at the bottom of a dish. Cut the sweetbreads into small pieces, and place them in the dish, then add some artichoke bottoms, truffles, asparagus tips, fresh mushrooms, and the yolks of hard-boiled eggs. Season with salt and pepper. Pour in some rich veal gravy; thicken with cream and flour. Bake in a moderate oven. Serve cold.

SHROPSHIRE PIE

Cover a dish with a good puff-paste. Chop together a rabbit and 1 pound of fat pork; season with salt and pepper; lay the rabbit and pork in the dish. Parboil the liver of the rabbit, and beat in a mortar together with the same quantity of bacon and a few sweet herbs; season with salt, pepper, and nutmeg; mix it with the yolk of an egg; make into balls and throw into the pie, adding to it a pint of white wine and some nutmeg. Bake in a quick oven for an hour. Serve cold.

SWEET PATTIES

Chop the meat of a calf's foot, boiled, together with 2 apples, an ounce of candied orange and lemon-peel, some fresh peel, and lemon-juice; mix with grated nutmeg, the yolk of an egg, a spoonful of brandy, and 4 ounces of currants. Fill the patty-cases, bake, and serve cold.

TURKEY PATTIES

Mince some of the white meat of a turkey, and season with lemon-peel, nutmeg, salt, pepper, cream, and a little butter; place over the fire, and thicken with a little flour. When cold, fill the patty-cases and serve.

VEAL PIE

Chop a little ham, some cold veal, and beef suet together with an onion, some parsley, lemon-peel, salt, nutmeg, mace, paprika, and bread crumbs. Bind with an egg or two. Fill the patty-cases; place in a quick oven. Serve cold.

Fish Patties

OYSTER PATTIES

BOIL 2 dozen oysters, strain, bread, and cut them into small pieces; place in a stewpan with 1 ounce of butter rolled in flour, half a gill of cream, grated lemon-peel, and half the oyster liquor; season with paprika, salt, and lemon-juice. Stir over the fire for five minutes, and fill the patty-cases.

LOBSTER PATTIES

Boil a lobster, pick out the meat from the tail and claws, chop it fine, place in a stewpan with a little of the spawn pounded in a mortar till perfectly smooth. Add 1 ounce of fresh butter, half a gill of cream, paprika, salt, a teaspoonful of anchovy essence, a little flour and water. Stew for

4

five minutes. Fill the patty-cases, and allow to cool.

PRAWN PATTIES

To 1 pint of broth add a tablespoonful of anchovy sauce, pepper, salt, and some grated nutmeg; boil for ten minutes, then add a little roux; boil and thicken. Add a pint of prawns; let come to a boil; when cold fill the patty-cases. Garnish with parsley.

SALMON PATTIES

Take half a can of salmon ; flake and mix with half a pint of cream thickened with a spoonful of butter rolled in corn-starch; season with salt, pepper, anchovy sauce, and a few olives chopped fine. Allow to cool, and fill the patty-cases.

Cold Sauces and Dressings

THERE is nothing more disagreeable to the palate than the taste of cold grease or fat; bearing this in mind, the cook will always remove the fat from the sauces.

In making dressing for salads it is always necessary that all the ingredients should be thoroughly incorporated before the dressing is added to the salad. To obtain this result satisfactorily it is necessary to mix the dressing in a cool room, and to have all the ingredients as cold as possible. When the dressing has assumed the proper consistency it should be placed on the ice until the very moment of sending to the table.

ALBERT DRESSING

Mix well 4 tablespoonfuls of olive - oil,

1 tablespoonful of wine, 1 tablespoonful of cider vinegar, a little paprika, and salt to taste. Place on the ice till wanted.

ASPIC SAUCE

Rub smooth the yolks of three hard-boiled eggs; add 1 ounce of salt, a quarter of a pint of oil—by degrees—till it becomes thick; then add 1 teaspoonful of anchovy essence and 2 tablespoonfuls of tarragon vinegar. Mix well and set on the ice.

CREAM DRESSING

To the juice of 1 lemon add 2 tablespoonfuls of drawn butter, 1 teaspoonful of French mustard, the beaten yolks of three raw eggs, 2 tablespoonfuls of cream, and salt to taste; beat smooth and set in a bain-marie until it becomes a thick cream.

CUCUMBER DRESSING

Remove the seeds from two large cucumbers; grate and drain; add to them 1 tablespoonful of finely chopped fresh red pepper, and mix with half a pint of mayonnaise dressing.

DUTCH SAUCE

Grate a cupful of horseradish; boil in a quarter of a pint of water; strain the water into 3 ounces of butter rubbed smooth with 3 ounces of flour; add to the horseradish, and stir to a smooth paste; add 2 table-spoonfuls of cream, and the yolks of 6 eggs well beaten, with 3 tablespoonfuls of cider vinegar; salt to taste.

GREEN SAUCE

Take equal quantities of tarragon, chervil, and cress; wash well; add the yolks of 4 hard-boiled eggs and 2 anchovies; pound all the ingredients well in a mortar; strain through a very fine sieve, and add olive-oil and lemon-juice as in making mayonnaise; season with pepper, salt, and mustard.

HORSERADISH SAUCE

Wash and scrape clean a large root of horseradish; grate fine. Put in a dish, and add 2 teaspoonfuls of sugar, 3 tablespoon-fuls of stock, 2 tablespoonfuls of vinegar, and salt; mix well together until the sugar is dissolved. This sauce will keep good for two or three weeks.

MINT SAUCE

Wash, pick, and mince the mint; place in a sauce-bowl with some sugar and vinegar; stir until the sugar is dissolved.

MAYONNAISE DRESSING

Chill the yolk of a raw egg on ice; then put the yolk on a very cold plate, and add a little salt and a gill of olive-oil, drop by drop, stirring constantly in the same direction; when it forms a cream, add a teaspoonful of French mustard and a tablespoonful of cider vinegar; stir all the time to keep from curdling. Lemon-juice or tarragon vinegar may be used instead of the cider vinegar.

MINT AND PARSLEY SAUCE

Take equal quantities of mint and parsley; mince, and add melted butter, a little lemon-juice, and salt to taste.

NETHERLAND SAUCE

Put 6 tablespoonfuls of cider vinegar in a

saucepan; allow to boil until reduced to half the quantity; when cold, add the yolks of 3 eggs, well beaten, a little nutmeg, and 5 ounces of butter. Place on a slow fire until thick, stirring constantly; then put in a bain-marie, add 3 ounces of butter, and beat to a froth. Cool on ice.

PLAIN OR FRENCH DRESSING

Mix well together 3 tablespoonfuls of olive-oil, 1 tablespoonful of vinegar, salt, and a little pepper. Keep cool until wanted.

RAVIGOTE SAUCE

Mince together cresses, chervil, tarragon, a few celery stalks, and 2 bay-leaves; add a tablespoonful of capers, 2 anchovies, salt, and pepper; pound all the ingredients in a mortar, and add the yolk of a raw egg, a little oil, and vinegar; beat to a cream, and add a little mustard.

SALAD DRESSING

Take the yolks of 2 hard-boiled eggs, a teaspoonful of grated Parmesan cheese, 1 teaspoonful of tarragon vinegar, mustard, and a teaspoonful of catsup; mix well, and add 4 tablespoonfuls of oil, and 1 tablespoonful of cider vinegar; beat the whole to a cream.

SAUCE FOR COLD MEATS

Grate a cupful of horseradish; add a tablespoonful of sugar, and cover with vinegar; add salt and a tablespoonful of French mustard.

SAUCE FOR FISH

Pound a tablespoonful of grated horseradish, 4 shallots, a clove of garlic, a salt-spoonful of mustard, and one of celery salt; add a little paprika. Pound well, and mix with half a pint of cucumber vinegar and a quarter of a pint each of shallot and horseradish vinegar. Let stand for three or four days; strain, and bottle the liquor.

TARTAR SAUCE

(1.) Mince 2 shallots, a little chervil, and tarragon; put in a vessel with mustard, a glassful of vinegar, salt, pepper, and a little oil; stir constantly. If too thick, add a little vinegar.

(2.) Chop fine, and add 4 or 5 olives, a gherkin, and a tablespoonful of capers to half a pint of mayonnaise dressing; mix well and serve.

VINAIGRETTE SAUCE

Mix together thoroughly 2 tablespoonfuls of olive-oil, 2 tablespoonfuls of cider vinegar, salt, and a little paprika; add a tablespoonful of finely chopped parsley, and 2 finely chopped olives.

Salads

LETTUCE, cresses, parsley, etc., are always used in salads; if not in their composition, they are used to garnish the dish, and, of course, should be as crisp as possible. Salad greens should be kept on ice, so that they will retain their freshness.

Before making the salad the greens should be picked and placed in cold water until ready to use, when they should be thoroughly dried and placed in the dish.

AMERICAN SALAD

Wash and pick 1 quart mixed salad; let drain; dry with a cloth. Cut very fine, and place in a dish, making a hollow in the centre. To 2 eggs add 1 teaspoonful of made mustard and salt; beat well, and add half a cup of oil and the same quantity of vinegar. Stir in half a cup of cream; pour the sauce over the salad. Cut two apples in thin slices, lay them around the salad, and garnish with beet. Bone 6 sardines and cut them lengthwise; take each half and roll up in a strip of lettuce, and stand them in the centre of the salad.

ANCHOVY SALAD

Remove the bones, heads, and tails of 6 anchovies. Wash two heads of lettuce, cut them small, and place on a dish. Add 6 button onions chopped finely, parsley, sliced lemon, and anchovies. Pour over the juice of a lemon mixed with a tablespoonful of oil.

CRAB SALAD

Boil 25 hard-shell crabs for about twenty or twenty-five minutes. When cool remove the top shell and tail; quarter the remainder, and pick out the meat carefully with a fork. The large claws should not be overlooked, nor the fat which adheres to the shell. Cut up an amount of celery equal in bulk to the crab meat; mix both together with a plain salad dressing. Put in a salad-bowl, and mask with a mayonnaise dressing; garnish with crab claws, shrimps, and hard-boiled eggs.

COD SALAD

Soak the cod overnight. Boil separately potatoes, carrots, and onions; chop fine, and add to the cod, which has been previously cooked and shredded. Make a dressing of 1 beaten egg, chopped parsley, fresh marjoram, oil, vinegar, salt, and pepper to taste. Pour the dressing over the salad and garnish with rounds of hard-boiled egg.

SALMON SALAD

(1.) Cut up a pint of cold boiled potatoes. Take equal quantities of cabbage, cucumber pickles, and canned salmon sufficient to make, after chopping, a pint in all. Chop the cabbage and pickles together, very fine. Remove all bits of bone and skin from the salmon, and pick into pieces. Mix together with the yolk of a hard-boiled egg, salt, and half a teaspoonful of dry mustard, 2 tablespoonfuls of oil, and 4 of vinegar; when smooth stir into the cabbage and cucumber, then stir in the potatoes and fish, and serve.

(2.) Chop 3 cold boiled potatoes and mix with 1 can of salmon; rub smooth the yolks of 3 hard-boiled eggs; season to taste with mustard, pepper, and salt; add 2 tablespoonfuls of cream and 4 of vinegar. Pour over the fish and potatoes.

(3.) Place in a salad-bowl 6 stalks of celery, sliced, and 1 pound of canned salmon; arrange neatly; add mayonnaise dressing, and garnish with parsley and rounds of hard-boiled eggs.

(4.) Take cold salmon cut into squares; dress in a dome in the centre of the dish, mask with a mayonnaise dressing, sprinkle whole capers over it, and encircle the base with rounds of hard-boiled eggs, and around this wreathe lettuce-leaves.

SARDINE SALAD

(1.) Take 3 heads of lettuce, 1 box sardines, 1 egg, half a cup of milk, half a teaspoonful of mustard, seasoning, a little roux, 1 tablespoonful of vinegar, 1 teaspoonful of anchovy paste, a pinch of sugar, and a boiled potato. Put the milk and seasoning in a pan with enough roux to make a thick sauce; let cool, and add to it the vinegar, mustard, anchovy paste, and half the oil of the sardines; mix well, and keep in a very cold place. Wash and dry the lettuce, place on a dish, and press together with the hands, and add the potato, cut small; pour the sauce over it; lay the sardines on this, and ornament with the yolks of hard-boiled eggs passed through a sieve, and the whites chopped fine; finish with rings and diamonds of beets.

(2.) Take 6 sardines, remove the skin and bone, and pour lemon-juice over them. Place in a salad-bowl with a crisp head of lettuce; chop up 2 hard-boiled eggs, add to the fish, and serve with a plain dressing.

BEEF SALAD

Cut into pieces an inch in length half a pound of cold meat; take 2 heads of lettuce, and wipe on a smooth cloth; place them in a salad-bowl; add the beef. Chop up a sweet Spanish pepper and add to the salad. Prepare a plain dressing, pour it over the salad, and mix gently.

ITALIAN CHICKEN SALAD

Make a dressing of the yolks of 3 hard-boiled eggs pounded fine, equal quantities of mustard and paprika, a pinch of powdered sugar, 4 tablespoonfuls of oil, 2 tablespoonfuls of vinegar. Simmer over the fire, but do not allow to boil. Take the white meat of two chickens, and separate into flakes; pile it in the middle of a dish, and pour the dressing over it. Cut up two heads of lettuce, and arrange around the chicken. On top of the lettuce place the whites of the eggs, cut into rings, and lay so as to form a chain.

RABBIT SALAD

Cut up the meat of 2 roast rabbits; place in a bowl and cover with a plain dressing; add a teaspoonful of minced salad herbs, and let stand for four hours. Put in a salad-bowl 3 heads of lettuce; drain the meat and add to the lettuce. Put into a plate 1 teaspoonful of French mustard; thin with 1 tablespoonful of the dressing taken from the meat, and add slowly to this 1 pint of mayonnaise dressing, and pour over the salad.

RUSSIAN SALAD

Chop and mix carefully together 2 ounces of roast chicken, and the same quantity of ham, beef-tongue, beef, and mutton, 4 truffles, 12 anchovies, 3 stalks of celery, 2 heads of lettuce. Mix with 8 tablespoonfuls of sauce tartare, and serve.

SALADE DE VEAU

Take some cold veal, mince, and soak in oil and vinegar for two hours. Put into a bowl with 1 teaspoonful of mustard and 2 teaspoonfuls of pounded anchovies; add some oil, vinegar, chopped parsley, chopped pickles, and whole capers, pour over the veal and serve.

SALPICON DE CARNE

(1.) Cut equal portions of cold meat and cold boiled potatoes into half-inch cubes; mix well, and dress with plain salad dressing, adding chopped parsley and fresh marjoram. Over this place rounds of onions which have been previously soaked in vinegar for two hours.

(2.) Cut cold meat into half-inch cubes; boil and chop an onion and add to it the meat. To this add olives, fresh marjoram, and parsley. Dress with a plain salad dressing and serve.

SALPICON DE GUATITAS

This is made in the same manner as the preceding receipt, using tripe instead of the meat.

ASPARAGUS SALAD

Drain 1 can of asparagus tips; throw into

5

cold water; drain again immediately, and wipe dry. Put into a salad-bowl, and pour over it French dressing.

BEET SALAD

(1.) Choose 6 large beets; bake them in a slow oven; peel and cut into small squares. Peel and cut into rounds 6 button onions, pour boiling water over them, and allow to stand for ten minutes. Throw off the water and repeat. Mix in a salad-bowl with the beets and chopped parsley. Pour French dressing over it and serve.

(2.) Cut into thin slices 4 small beets; boil 2 white onions, cut fine; add to the beets, and serve with a mayonnaise dressing.

BREAD SALAD

Cut into pieces about half an inch square a stale loaf of bread; chop equal parts of cold boiled potatoes, tomatoes, and cucumbers; season with a little grated onion, 1 tablespoonful of oil, the juice of 2 lemons, pepper and salt, and chopped parsley; mix with the bread; let stand for a quarter of an hour before serving.

CABBAGE SALAD

(1.) Cut a small cabbage as if for cold slaw. Make a dressing of the following ingredients : 3 eggs, 6 tablespoonfuls of cream, 3 of melted butter, half a teaspoonful of pepper, salt to taste, 2 tablespoonfuls of made mustard, 1 cup of cider vinegar; stir well together, all but the cream, and cook over the fire until they come to a boil. Set the dressing aside to cool; when cold add the cream, and pour over the cabbage.

(2.) Take a small cabbage and shred; add 4 stalks of celery chopped fine. Place in a salad-bowl and pour over it a pint of mayonnaise dressing. Garnish with parsley.

(3.) Chop up the cabbage quite fine ; place in a saucepan and pour boiling water over it, and add a little salt. Let stand for half an hour; wash in cold water and dry thoroughly; when dry place in a salad-bowl and add hard-boiled eggs and parsley chopped fine.

Serve with plain salad dressing and add some olives.

Carrot salad is made in the same manner as described in the preceding receipt.

CAULIFLOWER SALAD

(1.) Boil the cauliflower; when cold tear apart, dry on a soft cloth, and put in a salad-bowl. Pour over it half a pint of mayonnaise dressing. Garnish with lettuce-leaves and rings of hard-boiled eggs.

(2.) Boil the cauliflower until cooked, being careful not to overdo it. Chop it fine, and add chopped hard-boiled eggs and parsley. Garnish with olives and beets cut in fancy shapes. Pour French dressing over all.

CRESS SALAD

Take equal parts of cresses and celery stalks; cut up, place in a salad-bowl, and sprinkle with sweet herbs; pour over this a mayonnaise or plain dressing and serve very cold.

EGG-PLANT SALAD

Boil the egg-plant until cooked; peel and

cut into small pieces; add the juice of a lemon, 1 tablespoonful of oil. Mix well and serve.

GERMAN SALAD

Boil a cauliflower in well-salted water until quite tender. When sufficiently cooked place in a sieve to drain. When cold divide the cauliflower into small pieces. Mask with mayonnaise dressing and garnish with beets cut into fancy shapes.

GRAPE-FRUIT EN MAYONNAISE

Wash and dry 2 heads of lettuce, and make a nest in the salad-bowl; sprinkle over a little oil and vinegar, and season with salt and pepper. Peel the grape-fruit and separate into sections; split the membrane so that the pulp of the fruit can be extracted; separate into small bits and toss into the prepared nest. Mask with mayonnaise dressing and set in a cool place.

JARDINIÈRE SALAD

Take equal quantities of cold cooked potatoes, turnips, string-beans, beets, celery, and tomatoes. Put in a salad-bowl, and add chopped pickle, hard-boiled eggs, olives, capers, and shred lettuce; pour over a mayonnaise dressing, and garnish with lettuce-leaves.

KALE SALAD

Strip the inside leaves from the kale, place in a salad-bowl, and pour over the whole a French dressing. Garnish with cresses.

LENTIL SALAD

Cook the lentils in salted water, and drain. Put the lentils in a bowl, and add 1 chopped onion; stir in 1 tablespoonful of chopped parsley; add some chopped egg and shred lettuce; season with salt, pepper, oil, and vinegar, and decorate with parsley.

LIMA-BEAN SALAD

Boil the Lima beans in water with a little salt, a bunch of parsley, and an onion until quite tender; drain. Mix with 2 tablespoonfuls of oil, 4 tablespoonfuls of vinegar, a little chopped thyme and mint. Serve quite cold.

LETTUCE SALAD

Wash the lettuce thoroughly in cold water and dry with a soft cloth. Separate the leaves with the hand; otherwise they will become flabby. Place in a salad-bowl and dress with French or mayonnaise dressing.

PEA SALAD

Cook the pease in salted water; when done put aside to cool. Add to them a hard-boiled egg and a boiled white onion, chopped fine. Pour over them a dressing made of oil, lemon-juice, and salt and pepper to taste.

PERSIAN SALAD

Cut cold boiled potatoes into slices a quarter of an inch thick. Arrange in a salad-bowl and place on the ice. Chop 2 hard-boiled eggs; add 1 teaspoonful of minced parsley, a little chervil, 1 teaspoonful of salt, pepper, 4 tablespoonfuls of vinegar, and 8 tablespoonfuls of oil. Mix thoroughly and pour over the potatoes; stir together, and serve.

PRINCE SALAD

Cut a pint of cold boiled potatoes into small squares; add the same quantity of pickled cauliflower, minced fine. Mix 4 tablespoonfuls of vinegar, 1 tablespoonful of celery salt, 1 teaspoonful of made mustard, and 1 ounce of butter. Heat to the boiling-point; pour hot over the potatoes and cauliflower, stir lightly, and serve very cold.

SALADE ANDALOUSE

Chop fine 1 Spanish onion and a large cucumber; peel 3 tomatoes, cut into small pieces, take out the seeds, and strain the juice from them. Dress in a salad-bowl with salt, pepper, oil, and vinegar, and let stand for an hour. Make a mound of grated bread crumbs, all white, and arrange the salad above it, following the shape. Garnish with laurel-leaves and olives.

SALADE DE CRESSON

Take fresh tomatoes of a bright red, remove the seeds, pass the pulp which comes from the seeds through a sieve. Blend with this liquor the yolks of 2 boiled eggs mixed with the yolk of a raw egg, and add salt, pepper, and mustard. Take the watercresses, carefully cleaned and picked; dress and season each separately; then blend the two well. Do not mix until just before serving. Surround the tomatoes and cresses with lettuce-leaves. Pour a mayonnaise dressing in the centre.

SALADE DES HARICOTS BLANCS

Cook and strain white beans, and season with oil, vinegar, salt, pepper, a tablespoonful of cream, a tablespoonful of French mustard.

SPINACH SALAD

Place a quart of spinach leaves in a salad-bowl with a Spanish onion cut up fine and a little mint. Pour over half a pint of plain salad dressing, and garnish with hard-boiled eggs.

STRING-BEAN SALAD

(1.) String a pint of beans; boil in salt water with an onion and a sprig of parsley.

Place the beans in a salad-bowl, sprinkle with minced salad herbs, pour over a plain dressing, and serve very cold.

(2.) Cut the beans in four; place in a saucepan with cold water, and put on the fire; when the water comes to a boil the beans will be cooked; let cool. Dress with a plain salad dressing. A little boiled onion may be added.

SWEET-POTATO SALAD

Boil 3 large sweet-potatoes; cut into squares; add 2 stalks of celery, cut small. Pour over the following dressing; 3 table-spoonfuls of oil, 2 of vinegar, and salt and pepper to taste. Garnish with olives and parsley.

Creams

APRICOT CREAM

PUT 10 apricots in a pan with a gill of water and 5 ounces of sugar; cook; when done allow to cool; beat half a pint of cream very stiff, add the apricots passed through a very fine sieve, and 4 ounces of sugar; dissolve half an ounce of isinglass in a little hot water, mix with the cream, stir well, and pour into a mould.

BANANA CREAM

Take 5 bananas, skin and pound them to a pulp together with 5 ounces of sugar; beat half a pint of cream to a stiff froth; add the bananas, half a glass of brandy, and the juice of two lemons; mix well; add half an ounce of isinglass dissolved in a little hot water, beat for a few minutes, fill the mould, and set in a cool place.

CAVALIER CREAM

Melt 2 ounces of chocolate in half a gill of milk; beat three-quarters of a pint of cream to a stiff froth, add 8 ounces of sugar, half a glass of maraschino, the chocolate, the juice of 2 lemons, and a box of gelatine dissolved in half a gill of boiling water; mix well; pour into a mould, and stand on the ice to set.

CREAM À LA CARDINAL

Pick and clean a quart of raspberries; put them in a basin, add half a pound of sugar, bruise with a wooden spoon, and pass through a fine sieve; mix the pulp with a pint of cream, a few drops of carmine, and a box of gelatine dissolved in a small quantity of boiling water; stir well, pour into a wet mould, and stand on the ice till quite firm; serve with a custard poured over it.

EBONY CREAM

Stew 2 pounds of French prunes in a little

water; pass them through a sieve; add half an ounce of gelatine melted in a little water; a quarter of a pound of sugar; allow to boil; pour into a mould; when cold turn it out and serve with whipped cream.

HUNGARIAN CREAM

Put 1 pint of milk, half a pound of sugar, and 8 eggs into a pan; stir over the fire a few minutes; add half an ounce of isinglass; take from the fire and stand in a pan of cold water; add a glass of maraschino, 4 ounces of candied cherries, and half a cup of cream; stir till nearly set; pour into a mould, and stand on ice.

NORMANDY CREAM

Put half a pint of cream into a pan together with half a pint of milk, 1 box of gelatine, sugar to the taste, and a little vanilla; stir well; do not allow to boil; wet a mould, and arrange candied fruits in the bottom; pour in some of the cream, and set aside to cool; when firm lay in some more candied fruits and add more cream; repeat till the mould is quite full; place on the ice to set.

PINEAPPLE CREAM

Pour a little melted raspberry jelly in the bottom of a mould and allow it to set; soak a quarter of an ounce of gelatine in a gill of milk; stir it over the fire till thoroughly melted; beat a pint of cream to a froth; add a quarter of a pound of sugar and half a pound of chopped preserved pineapple; stir in the gelatine; when the raspberry jelly is set, pour in the cream.

PRUSSIAN CREAM

Beat half a pint of cream to a froth; add sugar to taste, and the juice of 2 lemons; beat 4 eggs; add to them a glass of maraschino; mix with the cream, and beat; stir in a little isinglass melted in water; have a mould standing in ice-water, pour a little of the jelly around it; sprinkle with blanched pistachios and candied cherries; when set pour in the cream, allow to set, and turn out on a dish.

Charlottes

APRICOT CHARLOTTES

BUTTER a mould. Cut a stale loaf into fingers, and a round the size of the bottom of the mould; fry them in butter and arrange them in the mould. Pare and stone a pound and a half of apricots; boil them with one pound of sugar for half an hour. Pour into the mould, cover with slices of bread dipped in butter, and bake in a moderate oven. Turn out on a dish and sift powdered sugar over it.

CHARLOTTE - RUSSE

Dip a mould in water; line it with small sponge - cakes; put glacé cherries on the bottom; mix a tablespoonful of sugar with a little lemon - juice and brandy. Add 2 tablespoonfuls of cream, and whisk to a stiff froth; stir in a little gelatine dissolved in milk. Fill the mould, cover with cake, and stand in a cool place to set.

CORNUCOPIAS

Mix well together 3 eggs, half a pound of sugar, half a pound of flour, 2 tablespoonfuls of water, 1 teaspoonful of baking-powder. Drop in tablespoonfuls on a pan, and bake in a moderate oven; when done, take out, and while still hot roll in the form of a cornucopia, and hold in shape till cold; fill the cornucopias with whipped cream.

GOOSEBERRY CHARLOTTE

Pick 2 pounds of gooseberries. Wash them well, and boil with half a pound of sugar until reduced to a pulp. Dissolve a little gelatine in half a cupful of hot water; mix it with the gooseberries, and pass them through a fine sieve. Line a mould with small sponge-cakes and pour in the gooseberries. Stand aside to set. Turn out on a dish, and serve with cream.

ORANGE CHARTREUSE

Make a quart of calf's-foot jelly, flavor it with orange, and keep in a liquid state; peel 4 oranges, and divide into small sections, being careful not to break the inner skin ; place the oranges in a flat dish and sprinkle powdered sugar over them, and set aside for two hours. Pour about a teacupful of the jelly into a plain mould; let set, and arrange upon it a layer of oranges ; pour over these some jelly; allow it to set; then some more oranges, and so on till the mould is quite full. When quite firm turn out on a dish, and surround the base with a border of whipped cream, and sprinkle the latter with chopped pistachios.

PINEAPPLE TRIFLE

Make small holes in a stale sponge-cake, and pour over it as much of the syrup of a pineapple as it will absorb; chop a few slices of the pineapple, put them around the bottom of the cake, and pour cream over the whole ; sprinkle with blanched almonds and pistachios cut very small, and candied cherries.

6

PORCUPINE

Put a pound of raspberries into a pan with a pound and a half of apples, pared, cored, and sliced; add enough powdered sugar to sweeten it, and boil on a slow fire till the apples are soft and pulpy; then pass through a sieve; stir in 2 ounces of dissolved gelatine, and pour into an oval mould; when firm turn out on a dish; stick it over with thinly cut almonds, to imitate the quills of a porcupine; pour over whipped cream and serve.

RASPBERRY GÂTEAU

Cut a sponge-cake into slices half an inch thick; place them in a dish; pour over them a pound and a half of raspberries and currants stewed with half a pound of sugar; allow to stand for half an hour; pile the cake in the centre of a dish; whip some cream to a froth; sweeten with sugar and flavor with wine; pour it over the cake, and send to the table.

STRAWBERRY CHARLOTTE

Line a mould with lady's-fingers; cover the bottom with a layer of jelly of some bright color. Make a filling as follows: put a pint of thick cream into a pan together with an ounce of dissolved gelatine and a pound of picked strawberries; mix thoroughly and pour into the mould; cover the top with some more fingers, place on the ice to set; serve with whipped cream.

Jellies

APRICOT JELLY

PLACE a tin of apricots in a pan with half a pound of sugar and allow them to boil; strain off the syrup; take out the kernels and remove the skin from the apricots; allow to cool; add to a pint of the syrup half a box of gelatine dissolved in a little water; boil, and clarify with the whites of eggs; pour a little jelly into the bottom of a mould, and when it is beginning to set place over it some of the apricots; add more jelly and apricots till the mould is full; set in a cool place, and serve with whipped cream.

CLARET JELLY

Mix together half a pound of powdered sugar, 1 bottle of claret, the juice and rind of a lemon, a small pot of currant jelly, and half a box of gelatine; boil for ten minutes; add a little brandy; strain, and allow to cool.

CHERRY JELLY

Soak a box of gelatine in a pint and a half of water; add the juice of 4 lemons, half a pound of sugar, and the whites of 2 eggs beaten in a little water; stir over the fire till it boils; pass through a jelly-bag until clear, then add half a glass of noyau, a few drops of essence of almonds, and color with a few drops of cochineal; pour into a mould.

MUSCAT JELLY

Soak 1 box of gelatine in water, add the juice of 2 lemons, half a pound of sugar, and the whites of 2 eggs beaten in a little water; place the pan on the fire and stir gently till it boils; take it up, and pass through a sieve till quite clear; stand in cold water, and when nearly set stir in a little elder-flower water and half a pound of muscatel grapes; pour into the mould, and stand aside to set.

ORANGE JELLY

Make a jelly the same as the claret jelly; free the oranges from the pith, and cut into small pieces with a sharp knife; when the jelly begins to set, stir in the oranges; place on the ice to set.

SANDRINGHAM JELLY

Soak 1 box of gelatine in cold water for an hour; add the juice of 3 lemons, half a pound of sugar, and the whites of eggs beaten in a little water; stir over the fire till it boils; let it settle, and pass through a jelly-bag till quite clear; add a glass of brandy, an ounce of pistachios, and a table-spoonful of boiled rice; stir the jelly till nearly set, then pour into the mould.

STRAWBERRY JELLY

Pour a little jelly into a mould, place a layer of strawberries over it, pour over some more jelly, and when set place over it another layer of strawberries; repeat till the mould is full, the last layer being of jelly.

TUTTI-FRUTTI JELLY

Put half a box of gelatine to soak in half a pint of cold water; dissolve in a pint of boiling water; add the juice of 3 lemons; three-quarters of a pound of sugar; strain; when it begins to set, put a layer of jelly on the bottom of a mould, then a layer of sliced bananas, then a layer of jelly, next a layer of sliced oranges, another layer of jelly, a layer of peaches; the last layer should be of jelly.

WINE JELLY

Soak half a box of gelatine in half a pint of cold water, then add a pint of boiling water, and stir till dissolved; add the juice of 3 lemons; strain; add some sherry, and when nearly set stir in a quarter of a pound of grapes, skinned and stoned; pour into the mould and set on the ice to harden.

ALMOND CREAM

(1.) BLANCH a half-pound of sweet almonds and a half-dozen bitter almonds. Pound to a paste in a mortar with a little water or milk to prevent oiling. Boil a quart of milk, pour it over the almonds and allow to stand until cold, when it must be strained through a cloth, squeezing it very hard to extract all the taste of the almonds. To this milk of almonds add a pint of cream and three-quarters of a pound of sugar, and freeze.

(2.) Blanch 1 pound of sweet almonds and roast them, being careful not to burn them. Pound them to a paste in a mortar with a little rose-water. Pour a quart of boiling milk over them, and allow to stand until cold, when they must be strained as in the preceding receipt. Now make a caramel of a half-pound of sugar, with which the cream is to be sweetened. To make the caramel put the sugar in a porcelain-lined saucepan with just enough water to moisten it, and place over a quick fire, being careful not to burn it. When the sugar is melted and of a delicate brown mix with a cup of boiling milk, stirring constantly until dissolved. Add this and a pint of cream to the milk of almonds. Freeze.

APRICOT CREAM

Mash 18 ripe apricots with a half-pound of sugar; add a quart of cream, and rub through a sieve. Add a few of the bruised kernels, and freeze.

BLACKBERRY CREAM

Make a custard of the yolks of 4 eggs and a quart of milk. Set aside to cool. Take a quart of picked blackberries and mash them with a half-pound of powdered sugar. Let it stand half an hour. Then strain, and add this juice to the custard, mixing it well. Add sugar to taste.   Freeze.

BISCUIT CREAM

Take half a dozen sponge biscuits and soak in a quart of cream; add the yolks of 3 eggs, well beaten, and a half-pound of sugar.   Put it over the fire to thicken, but do not allow it to boil.   Take from the fire and whisk until cold; add a spoonful of maraschino, and freeze.

BROWN-BREAD CREAM

Grate as fine as possible stale brown bread; take 2 tablespoonfuls and soak in a quart of cream for two or three hours, and sweeten to taste.   Freeze.

BURNT CREAM

Take a cup of sifted sugar; moisten and stir over the fire to a fine brown; add a pint and a half of cream; mix in the yolks of 4 eggs, well beaten, and 3 ounces of sugar. Place over the fire to thicken; do not allow to boil.   Take from the fire, whisk until cold, and freeze.

CHOCOLATE CREAM '

Take half a pound of chocolate and break in small pieces; melt it over the fire in a cup of water; add three ounces of sugar and a pinch of salt. When it is dissolved and well cooked add a quart of cream and a teaspoonful of essence of vanilla. Withdraw from the fire, whisk until cold, and freeze.

CINNAMON CREAM

Take an ounce and a half of the best powdered cinnamon and pour a quart of boiling milk over it. Let it stand for an hour, and strain through a thick cloth. Add 1 ounce of gum-arabic, dissolved in hot water, and sweeten with half a pound of sugar. Freeze.

COFFEE CREAM

(1.) To a quart of boiling milk add the yolks of 4 eggs, well beaten, and a half-pound of sugar. Place over the fire to thicken, but do not allow it to boil. Withdraw from the fire and mix with it a cupful of very strong coffee. When cold, freeze.

(2.) Take 4 ounces of freshly roasted coffee-beans and pour a quart of boiling milk over them. Allow to stand until cold; then strain through a napkin; add a half-pint of whipped cream and three-quarters of a pound of sugar. Freeze.

COCOANUT CREAM

Take a *fresh* cocoanut and grate it. Pour over it a quart of boiling milk. When cold, strain through a cloth, squeezing it very hard to get all the milk from the cocoanut. Add to this milk a half-pint of whipped cream and three-quarters of a pound of sugar. Freeze.

LEMON CREAM

(1.) Make a syrup of three-quarters of a pound of sugar and a cup of water; to this add the strained juice of 2 lemons and the grated rind of 1. Beat 4 yolks lightly and add to the syrup, stirring over the fire until it thickens. Withdraw from the fire, and when cold mix with a quart of cream. If not sweet enough, add more sugar. Freeze.

(2.) Beat well the yolks of 6 eggs; mix

gradually with this a quart of boiling water and the grated rind and juice of 2 lemons. Sweeten to taste, and stir this one way over the fire till it thickens, but do not let it boil. Add half a wineglass of sherry and a spoonful of brandy. Stir till cold, and freeze.

MELON CREAM

Take 2 good-sized muskmelons and cut the meat into small pieces. Cover with a pound of powdered sugar and stand in a cool place for an hour. Place over the fire, and cook for five minutes, taking care it does not burn. Pass through a sieve, and when cold mix with a quart of cream, and freeze.

MILLE FRUITS

Take a spoonful each of preserved strawberries, raspberries, apricots, currants, greengages, ginger, gooseberries, plums, and orange-peel cut into small pieces. Sweeten a quart of cream with half a pound of sugar; add to it a glass of noyau and the fruit. Freeze.

ORANGE CREAM

Scrape lightly, with a pound of lump-sugar, the rinds of 6 oranges. To this sugar add 3 cups of water and the strained juice of the oranges. Place over the fire, and boil for five minutes. Beat lightly the yolks of 6 eggs, and mix with the syrup. Return to the fire, and whisk lightly until it thickens; take from the fire, and add a glass of orange-flower water. When cold, freeze.

PINEAPPLE CREAM

Grate a fresh pineapple, and mix with a pint of syrup made from one pound of sugar. Add to this a quart of cream, and rub through a sieve. Before grating the pine take from it two or three slices, which must be cut into small dice and added to the strained cream before freezing.

PISTACHE CREAM

Beat to a paste in a mortar a half-pound of pistache nuts with a spoonful of brandy. Mix with a quart of cream and the yolks of 4 well-beaten eggs. Sweeten with half a pound of sugar, and place the mixture over the fire, stirring gently until it thickens. When cold, freeze. If you wish to color this cream, put to it a spoonful of spinach-juice.

RASPBERRY CREAM

Rub a quart of the fruit through a hair sieve to extract the seeds; then mix with a quart of cream, sweeten with half a pound of sugar, and freeze.

RATAFIA CREAM

Take 4 ounces of ratafia biscuits; pour over them 2 spoonfuls of noyau, the same quantity of sweet wine, the strained juice of a lemon and an orange. Sweeten with half a pound of powdered sugar, and beat the mixture with a quart of cream. Freeze.

TEA CREAM

Pour a quart of boiling milk over an ounce of tea-leaves and cover for five minutes. Strain in a bowl over a caramel made of 2 ounces of sugar. Beat the yolks of 8 eggs with half a pound of powdered sugar and a pinch of salt. Mix with the milk and place the whole over the fire, stirring gently until it thickens. When cold, freeze.

GINGER CREAM

Take 4 ounces of preserved ginger cut into small slices, 2 spoonfuls of the ginger syrup, 4 yolks of eggs, and a quart of cream. Place over the fire till it thickens, but do not boil. Sweeten with half a pound of sugar; whisk until cold, and freeze.

SPANISH CREAM

Boil 2 quarts of milk with a pound of sugar, the grated rind of a lemon and of an orange. Withdraw from the fire, and when cold add to it half a wineglass of orange-flower water. Freeze.

APPLE ICE

Pare and core 18 juicy apples; cut them into small pieces and cook in 3 pints of water with 2 slices of lemon-peel. When soft, pass the pulp through a hair sieve and sweeten with a pound of sugar; add the strained juice of a lemon. Set aside to cool, and freeze.

AURORA ICE

Beat in a mortar a half-pound of sweet and half an ounce of bitter almonds; mix the same with a quart of water and strain through a cloth. Make a syrup of a pound of sugar and boil pretty high; mix with almond water and boil until clear. Add the yolks of 4 well-beaten eggs, and stir gently until thoroughly mixed. When cold, freeze.

CHERRY ICE

Wash, pick, and stone two quarts of cherries; bruise them well; cover with a pound of powdered sugar and set aside for an hour. Then pour a quart of boiling water over them and strain through a cloth. Just before freezing add a glass of kirsch, if liquor is not objectionable, and a quarter of a pound of candied cherries cut in halves.

MUSKMELON ICE

Take the pulp of three good-sized melons and bruise well with a fork. Add to this a half-pound of sugar and set aside for half an hour. Then mix well with a quart of water

7

and pass through a cloth. Before freezing take the pulp of another melon, cut into small squares, and add to the mixture, with a very little grated nutmeg.

LEMON ICE

Make a syrup of a pound of sugar and a pint of water; boil in it 2 or 3 slices of lemon-peel. Take from the fire and add the strained juice of 6 lemons, a quart of water, and an ounce of gum-arabic dissolved in water. Before freezing take out the lemon-peel and add the whites of 2 eggs beaten to a froth.

ORANGE ICE

Make a syrup of a pound of sugar and a pint of water. Add to this the strained juice of 12 oranges, a wineglass of orange-flower water, and fresh water to make 2 quarts in all. Take 2 oranges, peel and separate in sections, from which take all skin and seeds, cut into small pieces, and add just before freezing.

PEACH ICE

Take a quart of ripe peaches, and pour

over them a quart of boiling water; allow them to stand only long enough to loosen the skins. Throw off the water and rub off the skins; cut into small pieces; cover them with half a pound of powdered sugar, and set aside in a cool place for half an hour. Pass through a hair sieve, adding a quart of water. If not sweet enough, add more sugar; if too sweet, a little lemon-juice.

PINEAPPLE ICE

Grate 1 good-sized pineapple or 2 small ones; add to the grated pine 3 pints of water, half a pound of sugar, and if the pine is very sweet the strained juice of 1 or 2 lemons. Strain through a cloth, and freeze.

STRAWBERRY ICE

Pick 3 pints of ripe berries; crush them with a silver fork, and cover with a pound of powdered sugar. Set aside in a cool place for half an hour, then add to the fruit 3 pints of water. Pass through a fine hair sieve or cloth, and just before freezing add a pint of picked berries.

WATERMELON ICE

Take the meat of a large ripe melon and mash it with a fork. Add to it a pint of water, a half-pound of sugar, the strained juice of a lemon, and half a teaspoonful of powdered cinnamon. Pass through a cloth, and freeze. If not sweet enough, add more sugar.

Cakes and Biscuits

ALMOND CAKE

BEAT to a cream half a pound of butter; add half a pound of powdered sugar, half a pound of currants, 4 well-beaten eggs, and sift in 4 ounces of powdered rice and 6 ounces of flour; butter a tin and fill with alternate layers of the paste and of the following icing: Pound to a paste one-quarter ounce of bitter and half a pound of sweet almonds; mix with the whites of 2 eggs and a little powdered sugar. The last layer should be of cake mixture; bake in a moderate oven.

CHERRY CAKE

Beat 4 eggs, and add 4 ounces of sugar and 6 ounces of flour; melt 4 ounces of butter over the fire, taking care that it is not too hot; add it to the mixture, stir in 4 ounces of preserved cherries cut in halves, and 1 teaspoonful of baking-powder; pour into a buttered tin and bake for about an hour.

DATE CAKE

Take 2 cupfuls of brown sugar, 1 cupful of molasses, 1 cupful of butter, half a cupful of sweet wine, half a cupful of milk, 3 eggs, 1 teaspoonful of cinnamon, 1 teaspoonful of cloves, a little nutmeg, 1 teaspoonful of soda, 1 pound of dates stoned and chopped, and enough flour to mix to a paste. Bake in a moderate oven.

NUT CAKE

Take 2 tablespoonfuls of butter, 2 cups of sugar, 2 beaten eggs, 1 cup of milk, 3 cups of flour, 1 teaspoonful of baking-powder, 1 pint of mixed nuts, blanched and chopped; flavor with vanilla. Put in a buttered tin and bake in a moderate oven.

PRINCESS CAKE

Take 6 eggs, half a pound of sugar, a quarter of a pound of pounded almonds, 6 ounces beaten butter, 6 ounces of flour, 2 tablespoonfuls of cream, and 1 tablespoonful of liqueur. Beat up the eggs with the sugar in a porcelain pot, set over a moderate fire, and continue beating; add the other ingredients one by one; stir in a cupful of stoned cherries. Take up from the fire, beat a little while, and bake in a well-buttered mould in a moderate oven.

RICE CAKE

Mix half a pound of sifted rice flour with half a pound of powdered sugar; add 6 well-beaten eggs; season with a little orange-flower water and a drop or two of essence of lemon. Beat the whole for twenty minutes, and bake in a quick oven.

SAVOY CAKE

Take 10 eggs, 1 pound of sugar, three-quarters of a pound of flour, the grated rind of a lemon, and a drop or two of essence of lemon. Beat the whites and the yolks separately; add to the yolks the sugar, and mix with the whites; stir in the flour, and put in the mould. Bake in a moderate oven for about an hour and a quarter.

SPONGE-CAKE

Beat the whites of 5 eggs to a stiff froth; beat the yolks well, and mix them with the whites; stir in half a pound of sugar and a third of a pound of flour; do not beat, as the cake will become heavy. Bake in a quick oven.

WHITE FRUIT CAKE

Take half a pound of flour, half a pound of sugar, half a pound of butter, half a pound of blanched almonds, one and one-half pounds of citron, half a grated cocoanut, the whites of 8 eggs, and 1 teaspoonful of baking-powder. Mix very carefully; put into a well-buttered mould, and bake in a slow oven for about two and a half or three hours.

ALMOND CAKES

Take 1 pound of flour, 1 pound of powdered sugar, 3 ounces of sweet almonds, and 2 ounces of bitter almonds, blanched and beaten; mix the ingredients well, together with the yolks of 3 eggs and the white of 1; butter the tin and place them in rough lumps.

BATH CAKES

Take 1 pound of flour, into which rub half a pound of butter, half a pound of sugar, 1 ounce of caraway seeds, 4 tablespoonfuls of brandy, 4 tablespoonfuls of sweet wine, and enough rose-water to make it into a paste; make it up into thin cakes, wash them over with rose-water, sift powdered sugar over them, and bake on a tin.

BRISTOL CAKES

Mix half a pound of flour with a quarter of a pound each of powdered sugar and butter, and 4 yolks and the whites of 2 eggs; when thoroughly mixed add half a pound of dried currants, and stir them well into the mixture. Butter a tin, drop the mixture from a tablespoon to form the cakes, and place in a brisk oven.

CINNAMON CAKES

Beat 6 eggs with a glass of rose-water; add a pound of powdered sugar, a quarter of an ounce of cinnamon, and enough flour to make a paste. Roll out and cut into small cakes; bake them on paper.

CRACKNEL

Mix 8 ounces of flour and 8 ounces of sugar; melt 4 ounces of butter in 2 tablespoonfuls of wine; make a paste with 4 beaten eggs; roll out as thin as paper, cut with a glass, moisten with the white of an egg, and dust with powdered sugar.

KENT DROP-CAKES

Take a pound of flour, half a pound of butter, half a pound of powdered sugar, and currants. Make into a paste with 2 eggs, 2 tablespoonfuls of orange-flower water, a glass of brandy, and one of sweet wine. Mix quickly, and drop the mixture through a funnel on the tins; bake for five or six minutes.

NUT CAKES

Beat 1 pound of walnuts with the whites of 3 eggs, add one and one-half pounds of sugar, mix well, and add the whites of 3 eggs; lay them out about the size of a nut, and cook in a slow oven.

QUEEN CAKES

Take 1 pound of sugar, 1 pound of flour, 1 pound of butter, 1 pound of currants, the yolks of 10 eggs, and 4 tablespoonfuls of brandy. Work it with the hand for half an hour, put into buttered pans, and sift powdered sugar over them. Place in the oven.

ROLL GINGERBREAD

Rub together half a pound of flour, a quarter of a pound of butter, a quarter of a pound of sugar, a teaspoonful of ginger, a teaspoonful of allspice, a teaspoonful of powdered cinnamon, the grated rind of a lemon, and as much syrup as will make it into a paste. Spread very thin on the tins and bake in a slow oven. When done cut in

squares, and while still warm roll it over a
stick till cold. Remove and keep in a dry
place.

SHORT CAKES

Rub into a pound of flour 4 ounces of butter, 4 ounces of powdered sugar, 1 egg, and
a tablespoonful or two of cream, so as to
make it into a paste. When mixed add currants to half and caraway seeds to the rest;
roll it thin, cut, and bake on tins.

BISCUIT DROPS

Take three eggs, 2 tablespoonfuls of rose-
water, a few caraway seeds; whip well together till it becomes a light froth; add half
a pound of flour; mix well and drop them
small; ice them with a little sugar, and bake.

CHOCOLATE BISCUITS

Add to 4 well-beaten yolks 2 ounces of
chocolate, scraped very fine, and 6 ounces
of sugar; mix well, and add the whites of 6
eggs beaten to a froth; when well mixed stir
in little by little 6 ounces of flour; put the
biscuit on white paper or in small paper

moulds; sprinkle a little powdered sugar over them, and bake in a moderate oven.

PALAIS-ROYAL BISCUITS

Take 1 pound of eggs, 1 pound of sugar, half a pound of flour; beat the whites and the yolks separately; stir the yolks into the whites; add the sugar, the grated rind of a lemon, and the flour; drop in square tins, sift powdered sugar over them, and bake in a quick oven.

Tarts and Pies

ALMOND CAKE

BLANCH and pound smooth 1 pound of sweet almonds with a little rose-water; stir in 3 well-beaten eggs, 2 ounces of warm butter, a little grated lemon-peel, a tablespoonful of lemon-juice, and 3 ounces of sugar; mix well. Line some patty-pans with puff-paste, put in the mixture, and bake in a quick oven.

ALMOND CUPS

Blanch and pound 1 pound of sweet almonds, adding a little rose-water; mix with three-quarters of a pound of powdered sugar; stir the paste over a gentle fire; make cups of the almond paste; bake them in a cool oven; when done, fill them with custard, and serve.

ANGELICA PIE

Take an equal quantity of peeled and cored apples and of angelica stalks, also peeled and cut into small pieces; boil the apples in water enough to cover them, to which add lemon-peel and sugar; boil some sugar till reduced to a syrup, and strain; place the syrup on the fire together with the angelica and boil for ten minutes; line a plate with puff-paste, over which put a layer of apples, then one of angelica, till the plate is full; pour in some syrup, put on the cover, and bake in a moderate oven.

LEMON TARTS

Mix together half a pound of powered sugar, 2 eggs, the crumbs of a sponge-cake, the juice and grated rinds of 2 lemons; beat smooth and place in tins lined with puff-paste; bake a light brown.

PEACH COBBLER

Line a dish with plain pastry, and pour into it freshly stewed peaches. Cover the dish with pastry, and bake a nice brown.

PRESERVED FRUIT PUFFS

Cut into squares a good puff-paste, and lay a small quantity of jam on each ; double them over and pinch the edges ; lay them on sheets of paper, ice them, and bake for about twenty minutes.

SANDWICH PASTRY

Roll out two pieces of paste very thin ; spread apricot or raspberry jam over one of them ; cover with the other, and bake ; cut it into squares and glaze.

SMALL PASTRY

Roll out a piece of puff-paste ; brush it over with egg ; sprinkle over it some chopped almonds and granulated sugar ; cut into shapes, and bake in a moderate oven.

SWEETMEAT ROLL

Roll a strip of puff-paste to an eighth of an inch in thickness ; spread with jam ; roll, and pinch the ends to keep the sweetmeats from coming out. Glaze with egg, and bake in a moderate oven.

Puddings

ALMOND PUDDING

BLANCH and pound very fine half a pound of sweet almonds. Beat up 8 eggs; mix 1 pound of sugar and three-quarters of a pound of butter to a cream; stir in the almonds, then the eggs; add a little rose-water and a pint of cream; place in a pudding-dish with a ring of puff-paste, and bake for three-quarters of an hour.

AMBER PUDDING

Beat together three-quarters of a pound of powdered sugar and 1 pound of butter till reduced to a cream; add the well-beaten yolks of 15 eggs, and enough candied orange to give it a color and to flavor it; line a dish with a crust the same as for pie, pour in the

8

mixture, cover it with crust, and bake it in a slow oven.

APRICOT PUDDING

Pass 6 ripe apricots through a sieve, and add 1 pint of cream, 4 ounces of sugar, 2 eggs, 4 yolks, and 1 ounce of melted butter; mix well, and bake in a dish lined with puff-paste, and glaze the top.

CARROT PUDDING

Grate half a pound of raw carrots and 1 pound of sponge-cake; mix the well-beaten yolks of 8 eggs and the whites of 4, together with half a pint of cream, half a pound of melted butter, half a pint of wine, 3 table-spoonfuls of orange-flower water, a grated nutmeg, and sugar; stir well, and if too thick add a little more cream. Lay a puff-paste over the dish, and bake it an hour.

DUTCH PUDDING

Mix 2 pounds of flour with 1 pound of butter melted in half a pint of milk; add the whites and yolks of 8 eggs beaten separately, half a pound of powdered sugar, a pound of currants, a few chopped almonds, and a little candied orange-peel; add 1 cake of compressed yeast; cover it, and allow to stand for an hour or two; bake in a wide flat dish for an hour.

GINGER PUDDING

Soak 12 sponge biscuits in a pint of cream, add the yolks of 10 eggs, 2 ounces of preserved wet ginger, cut in pieces, a spoonful of the syrup, and 2 ounces of melted butter; bake in a dish lined with tart paste, or cook in a bain-marie.

GOOSEBERRY PUDDING

Stew green gooseberries till they become a pulp, pass them through a sieve, and when cold add to them 6 ounces of butter, 4 ounces of sponge biscuit, powdered sugar to taste, 4 well-beaten eggs, and a glass of brandy; bake in a dish with a paste border.

JAM PUDDING

Mix together equal quantities of creamed butter, sugar, and raspberry jam, with 3 well-beaten eggs; nutmeg, cinnamon, and cloves to taste; bake in a paste-lined dish.

MACAROON PUDDING

Fill the bottom of a dish with macaroons, soak them in wine, and pour over them a custard made of 6 eggs, a pint and a half of cream, and a little milk; add to it candied fruits to taste; bake in a slow oven.

NORTHUMBERLAND PUDDINGS

Make a thick batter of flour and sweetened milk; when cold and firm beat it and add to it 4 ounces of melted butter, 4 ounces of currants, 2 ounces each of candied lemon and orange-peel, and a little brandy. Butter teacups, and bake the puddings in them; when done, turn out and allow to cool.

TRANSPARENT PUDDING

Beat up 8 eggs, place them over the fire in a bain-marie, and add half a pound of powdered sugar, half a pound of butter, and some grated nutmeg; keep stirring till it thickens; set in a basin to cool; place a puff-paste around the edges of a dish, pour in the mixture, and bake in a moderate oven.

WELSH PUDDING

Melt half a pound of butter in a bain-marie, and gradually add to it the beaten yolks of 8 eggs and the whites of 4; sweeten with powdered sugar, and season with lemon and nutmeg; bake in a dish bordered with paste.

Jams and Jellies

APPLE MARMALADE

PARE and cut the apples into small pieces; weigh and put them into a pan, adding half a pound of sugar to each pound of apples; add a stick of cinnamon and the juice of a lemon; place on a brisk fire; when the apples are reduced to a pulp, stir the mixture till of a proper consistence, and set aside to cool.

APRICOT CHEESE

Pare and stone the apricots, and place in a bain-marie; when soft pass them through a sieve; weigh the pulp, and allow three-quarters of a pound of sugar to each pound of pulp; place in a pan and stew for three-quarters of an hour.

APRICOT JAM

Pare and stone the apricots; sprinkle powdered sugar over them, in the proportion of a pound of sugar to each pound and a half of apricots, and allow them to stand for twelve hours. Blanch the stones, and put them with the fruit and sugar in a pan; allow them to simmer for an hour; take out the apricots; boil the syrup a little longer; remove the scum; put the apricots into the jars, and pour the syrup over them.

RASPBERRY JAM

Pick 6 pounds of raspberries; place them in a pan with a pint and a half of currant-juice; boil for twenty minutes; skim, and add 4 pounds of sugar; boil for an hour, being careful to remove the scum as it rises; put into jars, and cover.

STRAWBERRY JELLY

Allow 1 pound of sugar to every pint of strawberry juice. The juice should be boiled about twenty minutes before the sugar is added, and about fifteen minutes after it is added.

SANDWICHES should be very small and dainty, scarcely more than a mouthful, and always tastefully arranged on the dish. When sandwiches are rolled they should be tied with fancy ribbons and piled on the plate in log-cabin style; others may be cut into fancy shapes with cutters, such as stars, crescents, circles, etc.

ANCHOVY SANDWICHES

One sandwich loaf, 3 anchovies, 4 ounces of butter, 1 hard-boiled egg, seasoning, and a little nutmeg. Cut the loaf very thin; bone the anchovies, and pound them with the butter, egg, seasoning, and nutmeg; spread a little on each slice of bread, roll them, dish in a pyramid, and garnish with parsley.

ANCHOVY CREAM-TOAST SANDWICHES

Fry some slices of bread in boiling lard, dry and spread with anchovy paste; make a thick mayonnaise sauce, add to it some chopped capers, chervil, queen olives, and a bit of shallot. Spread on the fried bread, form into sandwiches, and serve with cresses.

AMERICAN SANDWICHES

Chop half a pound of ham very fine, together with 2 chopped pickles, mustard, salt and pepper to taste. Beat 6 ounces of butter to a cream, add the chopped ham, and mix well. Cut thin slices of bread, spread with the mixture, press together, cut into diamonds, and garnish with parsley.

CHICKEN CREAM SANDWICHES

Mix a cupful of white chicken meat and celery, chopped very fine, with a cup of milk. Add a boiled onion mashed, and thicken with 2 tablespoonfuls of corn-starch. It must be quite thick. When cooked and boiling, stir carefully into it the whites of 2 eggs beaten very stiff; add salt to taste. Place in a bain-marie; do not allow to boil. Stir in the juice of half a lemon and a tablespoonful of butter. Mould the day before; cut into slices and place between thin slices of buttered bread.

ÉLITE SANDWICHES

Take cold beef, boiled tongue, ham, and cold roast turkey in equal proportions; chop very fine, and stir well together in a bowl. Chop up pickled gherkins and stuffed olives. Make a salad dressing and pour over the whole; mix well, and place between thin buttered slices of bread.

FRENCH SANDWICHES

Chop 1 cup of white meat of a chicken, 3 olives, 1 gherkin, and a tablespoonful of capers; add half a pint of mayonnaise dressing, and thin with a tablespoonful of tarragon vinegar. Spread on thin slices of bread, roll, and tie with ribbons.

SAVORY SANDWICHES

Mince hard-boiled eggs very fine, spread evenly upon neatly cut pieces of buttered bread; grate over the egg a little prime cheese, add salt and paprika to taste.

SPANISH SANDWICHES

Bone 12 oil-preserved anchovies, and cut into strips about an inch long. Make into a paste with 1 ounce of capers and a sprig of parsley, adding a dash of paprika, half a teaspoonful of mixed mustard, 1 tablespoonful of tarragon vinegar, 1 tablespoonful of oil, the yolks of 2 hard-boiled eggs, and salt. Mix smooth; chop the whites of the eggs. Butter thin slices of bread, spread with the paste and sprinkle over them the chopped whites. Trim and tie with narrow colored ribbons.

SALMON SANDWICHES

One can of salmon, half a pint of mayonnaise dressing, 1 tablespoonful of capers, and a little chives. Chop the salmon, chives, and capers together very fine. Mix in the dressing, and spread on thin slices of bread.

SARDINE SANDWICHES

Chop together 6 boned sardines, 2 hard-

boiled eggs, 5 olives.   Mix well, adding some
of the oil of the sardines, lemon-juice, French
mustard, and salt.   Spread on thin slices of
bread, and roll.

PARISIAN SANDWICHES

A quarter of a pound of cooked beef
tongue, a quarter of a pound of lean ham, 2
ounces of butter, 3 truffles, seasoning, and
water-cress.   Pound the ham and tongue in
a mortar; when quite smooth add the seasoning, nutmeg, and butter; mix well together.
Chop the truffles very fine, and add them to
the mixture.   Spread on thin slices of bread,
sprinkle a few cresses over the paste, and pair.

TONGUE SANDWICHES

Half a pound of butter, 3 tablespoonfuls
of mixed mustard, 3 tablespoonfuls of oil, a
little paprika, salt, the yolk of 1 egg.   Mix
together very smooth and set on the ice.
Chop some ham and tongue in equal proportions, and blend all well together.   Cut the
bread very thin, spread with the mixture,
and roll.

TOOTHSOME SANDWICHES .

One pound cooked chicken, 4 ounces of butter, salt and pepper to taste, 1 teaspoonful of ground mace, half a nutmeg, and a slice of ham. Chop the chicken and the ham with the butter, add the spices, and pound to a paste. Spread on thin slices of bread, pile on a dish, and garnish with parsley.

VEAL SANDWICHES

To 1 cup of chopped veal and 1 hardboiled egg add 2 ounces of butter, 2 tablespoonfuls of catsup, salt and pepper to taste. Mix well, and spread on thin slices of bread.

VALENTINE SANDWICHES

Chop together 1 cup of chicken meat, 6 button mushrooms, add salt and pepper, and half a pint of mayonnaise dressing. Spread on thin slices of bread, cut into the shape of hearts, and garnish with parsley.

ZEPHYRETTE SANDWICHES

Rub to a paste 1 small Neufchâtel cheese, 1 ounce of butter, the yolks of 2 hard-boiled eggs, and half a teaspoonful of paprika. Mix with the whites of the eggs, and spread on zephyrette biscuits or on thin slices of bread.

THE END

REFERENCE-BOOKS FOR WOMEN

THE EXPERT WAITRESS. By ANNE T. SPRINGSTEED. 16mo, Cloth, $1 00.

OUR HOME PETS: How to Keep Them Well and Happy. By OLIVE THORNE MILLER. Illustrated. 16mo, Cloth, $1 25.

THE TECHNIQUE OF REST. By ANNA C. BRACKETT. 16mo, Cloth, 75 cents.

WHAT TO EAT : HOW TO SERVE IT. By CHRISTINE TERHUNE HERRICK. 16mo, Cloth, $1 00.

HOUSEKEEPING MADE EASY. By CHRISTINE TERHUNE HERRICK. 16mo, Cloth, $1 00.

CRADLE AND NURSERY. By CHRISTINE TERHUNE HERRICK. 16mo, Cloth, $1 00.

FAMILY LIVING ON $500 A YEAR. By JULIET CORSON. 16mo, Cloth, $1 25.

THE HOUSE COMFORTABLE. By AGNES BAILEY ORMSBEE. 16mo, Cloth, $1 00.

CHOICE COOKERY. By CATHARINE OWEN. 16mo, Cloth, $1 00.

MANNERS AND SOCIAL USAGES IN AMERICA. By Mrs. JOHN SHERWOOD. 16mo, Cloth, $1 25.

PRACTICAL COOKING AND DINNER-GIVING. By MARY F. HENDERSON. Illustrated. 12mo, Water-proof Cover, $1 50.

DIET FOR THE SICK. By MARY F. HENDERSON. Illustrated. 12mo, Cloth, $1 50.

MOTHERS IN COUNCIL. 16mo, Cloth, 90 cents.

MONEY-MAKING FOR LADIES. By ELLA RODMAN CHURCH. 16mo, Cloth, 90 cents.

PUBLISHED BY HARPER & BROTHERS, NEW YORK.

For sale by all booksellers, or will be sent by the publishers, postpaid, on receipt of price.